A Doll in Solitary

Dawn Blair

ALSO BY DAWN BLAIR:

Stonecharmer

Stonecharmer

Stonebreaker

Stonesinger

Onesong

Palladium

Tangled Magic

Walk the Path

Other darker tales

The Last Ant

Broken Smiles

Oxygen

Tree of Death

Give Up the Ghost

Riding Thunder

The Vigil

Red Cadillac Dreams

Author's Note

Before you start, we should talk. Have a seat. You'll want to be sitting down.

I want to give this account so that you may hopefully discern fact from fiction, a very tricky line.

The story you are about to read was inspired by the house I grew up in. It is in a small town, so everyone knows the house. It is a beautiful craftsman style house built around 1910. I adore the house, particularly the beveled glass French doors.

This story started as an assignment for a gothic writing class and the assignment was to write about that one spooky house from your hometown. Two houses popped into my head at once. One was not my house, but was so scary that I never dared to approach it. Someday, I will write about that house because there's still something to this day that holds me fascinated. One thing I can tell you is that every time I mention a dark forest in a book, rarely do they ever reach the level of dark forest that surrounds that house. It's in the middle of a town block, so I really don't know why it is that black. For many years, I didn't even realize there was a house back there. But that really is another story.

The other house was my house. The number of people that told me that my house was spooky was just about everyone I knew. Now, I will say that living in an old house is inherently spooky. They creak, pop, and make all sorts of weird noises. Cracks appear on the walls. Sometimes places in the floor aren't quite level. They settle in. But the idea of using my house as the basis for a story sounded thrilling.

I've had my share of unexplained and flat-out supernatural occurrences on the property where the house is. I've been told that a 3-year-old drowned in one of the ditches though I was also later in life told that it was false and I've never been able to find evidence of such a death happening. But if it didn't, I'd really like to know who pushed me into the ditch, tried to drown me, and kept my friend who was standing less than ten feet away from me from hearing anything until I had managed to pull myself up to safety. She didn't hear me hit the water, she didn't hear me screaming, she didn't hear branches of the tree breaking off as I tried to hold onto it to keep from going underwater which I knew was only waist deep but my feet weren't touching the ground. That is one true story I wish wasn't a true story.

However, let me stress that the events of this story are entirely made up. Well, there is supposedly a box of photos hidden somewhere. My nephews and I drove my brother crazy chasing stories of the box. Of course, he wouldn't let me go on the adventure. I think he's in on the conspiracy. So, if the box does exist, we have no idea what it really contains.

The best tales always contain elements of truth. The story of this mystery box and my house that inspired this one. Beyond that, none of it is true, and the box might not even exist. Until it is discovered, we are left to wonder what secrets it might hold.

I will keep you here no longer and will let you get to reading the tale.

Oh, I might also add that I've never liked dolls.

— DAWN BLAIR (2025)

A Doll in Solitary

I'D NEVER BEEN TO THE HOUSE BEFORE. MY CLIENT HAD always come to the office, and though the two places were literally right down the road from each other, it felt strange parking on the gravel just off the road beside the century-old house.

I knew the family used the driveway which ran beside the lawn which stretched alongside the house, but crossing between the two rectangular river rock pillars to enter the property felt too familiar considering I didn't know the family all that well aside from their legal matters. I felt more comfortable parking on the outside and crossing the bridge to go to the front of the house.

Two noble firs guarded the property as well, one sitting by the family's drive and the second on the other side of the bridge leaving a view of the grassy lawn going towards the craftsman style house.

For a long moment, I sat in my car just staring toward the house with its woodwork, glass, and stone. Even crossing the bridge felt imposing and my heart quickened with apprehension at the anticipating thought.

The corners of the bridge had four of its own river rock pillars, the forward two with rounded caps painted white and the back two with flat caps with large planters on them which I assumed were made of molded cement rather than stone though they had that look about them. Both containers were filled with sedum and tall ornamental grasses.

The broad cement walkway continued up to a short but equally wide cement staircase leading up to the craftsman house. Two more of the stone pillars sat at the front edge of the porch, each with planters of their own with bright pink and yellow begonias spilling over the edges. Two thick chains the size of my fist extended from the house to hold up the portico which covered most of the wide porch. At one time, the other half of the porch might have been used as a sundeck but there was no furniture there now.

Beneath the center of the portico was a heavy-looking mahogany front door with six little beveled diamond-shaped windows which seemed far too high up for anyone to look out of. One each side of the door was a large picture window with diamond lozenges at the top.

I noticed a dark movement behind the glass of the window and realized that someone had been standing there watching me, waiting.

I grabbed my purse and the black leather portfolio holding a fresh yellow legal pad and pen. I knew I had no reason to be nervous. I'd known this family, the Kjelgaards, all my life. But I'd also heard stories of the house. And it's haunts.

I'd never expected to be invited here.

It was time for me to get out of the car. I hadn't been sitting there long, long enough to be checking my hair and makeup if I'd felt the need to explain myself, but to me it felt like I'd been here hours already. I'd heard that time could get strange that way here.

I hadn't realized I'd parked in the shade of the nearest fir until I climbed out of my car and its shadow fell over me. It wasn't a warm spring day and I'm sure I shivered at the sudden chill I felt in the forest-scented air. I couldn't believe the pine fragrance the tree let off.

It felt wrong that I was here. It might have been because I didn't yet know why I was here. I'd been called by the wife of Mr. Jens Kjelgaard, my client, and asked to come straight away to the house. She hoped that I didn't have an appointment scheduled already, but if I did, I should cancel it because this was of the utmost importance and I would be compensated for it.

Fortunately, Little Grove takes after its name and not many matters of urgency happen here. I'd had no prior appointment or court appearance to be in conflict with a trip to visit a client. But I didn't often go to a client's house for more than to drop off paperwork or get a needed signature. If a client wanted to see me for a longer chat, I always made sure it was in my office. Lawyer or not, the world could be dangerous for a woman. I knew that better than some and had just set boundaries to safeguard myself automatically.

Was I here because a woman had called? If Mr. Kjelgaard himself had phoned for me, would I have agreed to come?

Probably. Mr. Kjelgaard was an old man with a friendly face and a pocketbook which didn't mind paying for good service. I'd felt a few of my bills had been extreme for the work he'd requested, but the invoices had always been paid with a prompt check and a cheery note thanking me for my fine legal mind. I figured he was just being a flirt as senior gentlemen can often be.

I would get in, figure out what they needed, and get out. Once I was back at my office, I'd probably laugh about the whole trip and what a scaredy cat I'd been. It was just a house, after all.

As I set my feet on the bridge, I tried to imagine this house being mine. It was well kept, beautiful, and aside from the hard look of the stones, there was nothing that should be menacing about it. The house was old, like the kindly Mr. Kjelgaard. I really couldn't under-stand why I'd have such instinctual fear about the place.

But I did have it, touching at the back of my neck like a ghostly warning that I shouldn't be there.

The Kjelgaards had few friends that they invited over to the house. Rumor had it that Jens' father Skold Kjelgaard had a frightful fear of being robbed, something stemming from his life in the old country of Denmark where the family originally hailed.

Little birds, mostly grackles, chirped merrily in the trees and accompanied the coos of mourning doves further away.

The bridge would have been a fine bridge if it didn't span a currently dry ditch. It was too soon for the irrigation water to be running, but farming season would be coming soon to the valley and every ditch would be filled. Right now, someone had come along to burn weeds and last fall's leaves from the ditch, leaving nature blackened and curled nearly to ash. A cat had walked through recently, probably stalking a mouse, and left tracks in the soot.

A neighborhood rooster crowed. The noise cut through the spring day and startled me as if someone had run nails on a chalkboard. I wanted to be back to the quiet of my office.

I broke from the shadow of the fir tree and walked through cool sunlight to the porch.

The figure at the window moved again. I couldn't tell if it was male or female, only a dark carrot shape of a person.

There was no railing on the staircase which fortunately I didn't need. I felt the chill the moment I was out of the sun and standing beneath the portico with its square support beams jutting out from the house.

Aside from the beams and the chains, nothing else supported the nearly free-floating overhang.

In the wood around the door, I saw there once had been a screen on the door, but now only the black, unfilled screw holes remained. If I thought about it hard, I recalled a fancy wooden screen door painted in dark green. I tried to remember when the outer door had been removed, but couldn't remember. Perhaps it had been while I was off at college becoming the brilliant legal mind that Mr. Kjelgaard thought I was.

I knew someone was right on the other side of the door even as I debated whether to knock on the hard wood of the door or to ring the old-fashioned metal doorbell. Did it even still work? Knowing there was someone right there, I opted for knocking. I would have rather that they just open the door and greet me, but the person didn't.

A tall, thin man dressed in a full suit and tie opened the door. He looked like someone dressed for court but I'd never seen him before and he was overdressed for Little Grove. I would have remembered someone like that. His lips tightened, thinned. "You must be the lawyer," he said, but it came out in a funny drawl like "laoy'er." I felt that he instantly disliked me.

"I'm Stephanie Hale, Mr. Kjelgaard's attorney." I emphasized the word "attorney." "Mrs. Kjelgaard called my office this morning and requested that I come immediately."

He snickered in a very unamused way. "Yes. Jens has

such a sense of humor. Can't even die without a little dramatic flair."

My breath hung on his statement. "I'm sorry. Is Mr. Kjelgaard dead. No one informed me of his passing."

This man, tall and thin in a suit, gave me a slow blink. "No, but there is a good chance he is nearly."

Well, that explained the strange call from the wife and the request to come to the house. I started to feel a little more at ease with the situation. At the end, many people wanted to make last moment updates to their wills.

I knew Mr. Kjelgaard's will had been updated not long ago because I'd done it when I'd first returned home to Little Grove after passing the bar exam. I'd had to remove a son who had died eight years previously.

"Steph!" came a shout from further inside the house. "Uncle Ivar, let her come in." There was an adorable roll to the R, and I had a distant memory of someone that had just a little of that accent. It was so long ago.

Ivar stepped back, swinging the door open a little more, and swept his arm as if formally inviting me into the house. The room I stepped into seemed like an elegant ballroom, though a bit small. It smelled of oily furniture polish. Chandeliers with six shaded bulbs hung from the ceiling on each end of the room, casting light upon the shining wooden floor. Off to one side of the room was a brick fireplace with a high wooden hearth. The brick showed signs of soot, showing that it did indeed see use though it was currently swept clean.

Mahogany wood paneling covered from floor to trim on the far wall. It darkened the room, but it matched the fancy rectangular beams that ran around the ceiling of the room. A dark leather sofa sat against that wall yet the puffy cushions looked like someone had been sitting there until recently. A smaller love seat sat along the wall opposite the fireplace. The space in the middle felt large and empty. The room would have made a beautiful home office with an elegant wood desk and big Queen Anne wing chairs for meeting clients.

A man, this one younger though also in a suit, entered through one of the two French glass doors with beveled panes which lead into the rest of the house. He beamed when he saw me and rushed over to greet me in a hug while I stood motionless, stiff, and finally gave him an awkward pat on the back.

He stepped back, now giving me an odd look. "You don't remember me, do you?" he asked.

He had blond hair and blue eyes that looked as if they could be water themselves and that clearly wanted me to recognize him as he did me. I flipped through all the people that I'd known in Little Grove growing up. So many people had moved away. But certainly I'd remember those eyes.

"Never mind," he said. "I was a few years younger so you probably didn't even know I existed."

I'd been flipping through my mental Rolodex the

wrong way. When I went backwards, I remembered a Kjelgaard a few years younger than me. "Ras?"

His smile grew brighter. "Ah, you did notice me." He looked like he could smack his hands together and do a cheery dance.

"This really isn't the appropriate time for cheer and laughter, Rasmus." Ivar said as he closed the door and walked around us.

Ras' mood grew quickly somber. "I'm sorry, Uncle Ivar. You're right." He stepped in close to me and whispered, "It's good to see you."

He turned and followed his uncle through the beveled glass doors into the living area of the house. I wasn't sure if I was to follow or not, but since I hadn't been told, I did. It was easy to follow Ras. He looked lean and elegant in suit and I had to quickly tamp down thoughts that weren't very professional of me to be thinking about the son of my client.

The drapes were closed in the living room, except for a small triangle where the heavy material got caught on the back of a brown padded and brass tacked wingback chair set clearly too close to the window. I couldn't tell, but if the curtains were an indicator, there was another plate glass window behind.

On each side of the wingback, there were ebony bookcases with leaded glass doors which matched the cupboards hanging over a serving hatch. I could barely see through to a kitchen and someone walking around on the other side of the wall. In the cupboards above, I saw crystal dishware which made me wonder if at one time this had been a dining room rather than a living space.

There was no other furniture in the room, and I briefly wondered if the couches had been pushed to the front room and everything else stored elsewhere.

Two women each in black dresses and their grey hair pulled back into tight buns stood with a little girl standing in front and halfway between them. The girl had on a dark blue dress and a bonnet which made her seem as if she'd stepped back into a time as old as this house. Each of the women had a hand on the child's shoulder.

I felt everyone staring at me. I tried to smile, but couldn't. The room felt too somber.

There was a door into the kitchen, half open so that I could see a knife block near a plate on a marble counter. Another door was closed to my left and on the opposite wall was a doorway into a dark hallway.

Uncle Ivar went first to close the service hatch. It rolled upwards from behind cabinets to reveal a mirror which reflected back the mostly barren room around us. Then, he went to the window and pushed the material off where it had caught on the chair, closing the curtain and darkening the room further.

I had a visceral reaction to the drape falling close that I didn't expect. I'd been in this house before even though I didn't remember it. I remembered so clearly the curtain being drawn shut and the way the light vanished from the room as it did now. The only light now in the room was from the chandelier which matched the two of the front room, a touch of sunlight coming through the smaller windows above the bookcases which had beige gossamer cloth over them, and the light which came through the double French doors of beveled glass. Even that seemed quite dampened. The little light that came in was a stark contrast to the dark.

"I'm sorry we have to have the curtains closed," Ras said. "We're a very private family."

She knew. She didn't even know Jens had a brother.

A long moan came from down the hallway. One of the women went and closed the door.

"Is that Mr. Kjelgaard?" I asked. "Does he need medical attention?"

"Jens does not need medical services. What he requires is you," Ivar said.

Chills prickled along my skin. "Is one of you Mrs. Kjelgaard?" I asked the women. I didn't like dealing with Ivar. Or maybe I'd have better luck with Ras, but as I turned to look for him, I saw him disappear behind another, this time singe, French door, one I'd not noticed when I first entered, but I had a vague memory of it.

When had I been here? More importantly, why had I repressed the memory of it? I wasn't the type of person who tamped down experiences and hid them away from myself because I couldn't deal with them. For that matter, I had no real trauma in my past, something that I had learned in my profession was very rare.

"Auntie, may I go play now?" the little girl asked,

looking up at the one woman who still held her shoulder. I wondered briefly if she could be Ras' child.

"You may get your doll," the woman said.

The girl clapped and went to the cabinet. She twisted the brass oval knob on the door and with a squeak the door opened for her. She reached in among the plates separated with tissue paper and pulled out a little doll with two blonde braids. Carefully closing the door, where she had to push it slightly and the wood once again protested, she turned to me as she hugged the doll close.

"She was bad and had to be put away in the solitary room," the girl told me before plopping down in the center of the room and rocking the doll. I heard her muttering about being good and not causing any more problems because she might be left in the solitary room for good.

Ivar took a seat in the wingback chair and crossed one leg over the other. His polished black shoe reflected a pinpoint of light coming from the chandelier.

I felt an uncomfortable itch rising across my shoulders as I stood there, the girl still rocking her doll near my feet and the eyes of the two remaining women staring at me. I wished Ras would come back into the room. I hoped he'd just run off to get something and that he'd return shortly. Like any time now.

I folded my hands over the top of my portfolio holding my yellow legal pad which I held down in front of me and turned toward Ivar. "Could you please explain to me why I've been brought here? I shouldn't be away from my office for too long. I told them I'd be right back." I also looked towards the women, still not knowing which of them was Jens Kjelgaard's wife, but wanting someone to give me an answer.

"I called your office and told them that we required your services and that it might take a day or two," one of the women said. "Surely they mentioned this to you when they relayed the call through to you."

"No, I wasn't informed." I wish I'd had more sharp irritation in my voice, but I couldn't muster it.

The girl turned the doll over and began to spank it. "You mustn't use that tone with people. It's not polite."

I wondered with a certain horrification if I'd been the reason the child spoke as she did.

"Helga, run along and play outside," Ras said as he came back into the room. He held a metal container smaller than a jewelry box.

The child leapt to her feet and ran through the kitchen dangling the doll from her hand.

"Don't get yourself dirty," the woman who wasn't Mrs. Kjelgaard shouted.

"I won't." A moment later, a door slammed, sending a shudder through the whole house.

"Kids," Ras said. Once again, it was his smile that put me at ease.

"Is she yours?" I asked as if we were the only two people in the room. I found myself holding my breath for his answer. A daughter might mean that he was married and, therefore, unobtainable.

His eyes twinkled. "She is Jens' child."

I didn't understand how that could be possible. Mrs. Kjelgaard was far beyond child-bearing years, even accounting for the child's age of somewhere around six to seven.

"One of my brother's nasty little secrets," Ivar said. He shook the foot of the leg crossed over his knee as if trying to shake off filth from his shoe.

It was Mrs. Kjelgaard I looked to next. I wanted to see her reaction to the way everyone spoke of her husband's infidelity. She looked unfazed by it. Was she used to it, or had the matter been so thoroughly discussed that it could be put to bed in the past? It seemed so strange to think that kindly Mr. Kjelgaard could be unfaithful or sinister.

But then, how well did she really know him outside her office? It's not like they ran into each other all the time, even with Little Grove being such a small place. Maybe he paid his bills so quickly and without complaint because he didn't want to draw attention to himself.

The room was starting to feel hot and stifled. I was having trouble breathing.

"I'd really like to know why I was called here," I said, trying to keep any weakness from showing in my voice. "But I feel this is a bad time. I shouldn't be here. I can get in touch with Hospice if you like. They can come in to help. Mr. Kjelgaard might find it comforting."

"Private family," Ivar muttered.

"I realize that, but at a time like this –"

"Rasmus," his mother said, "do tell me that you've prepared a place for the girl as you were asked.

"Of course I did. Right this way, Steph."

I hadn't paid much attention before when he'd called me by my shortened name, but now it seemed strange. Did he really feel that he knew me well enough to call me by an endearment? In the oppression of the room, I didn't know if I minded or if it seemed like the only lifeline I had to hold onto. It made me feel like if there was anyone in this house that wouldn't harm me, it would be Ras.

Ras turned and headed towards the door opposite the chair where Ivar sat. He opened it and I clearly saw that it was a bedroom. My feet hesitated to follow as Ras stepped inside.

"Come on," Ras urged with a tip of his head.

Another deep moan came from behind the closed door to the hallway. It left chills running down my back and I had half a mind to run for the French doors. Could anyone stop me if I bolted and ran from the house?

"I'll go check on him," Mrs. Kjelgaard said as she opened the hallway door only far enough to slip through and then closed it again behind her.

"I don't feel it's right for me to be here. I'm going to go," I said to Ras. "I'll be glad to see you all down at my office when things settle down."

"No, please, let me know you why we've called you here," Ras said.

I inhaled short, hesitant breaths. "I really don't think now is the time. You should be with your father."

"My father has asked that you be shown what's in this box," Ras said as he raised it to catch my attention. "He says you'll need to understand."

That was my client, dying and wishing for me to see the contents of the box before he passed. What I discovered in the box might be relevant to some legal matter he needed tended to. Had something happened in the last few days and the stress of it pushed him into his final days?

The curtains in the bedroom had also been drawn, but a light not quite as impressive as the chandeliers hung from the ceiling. The space was cast in a pale yellow from the soft white bulb in its shade. A full-sized bed took up most of the room, but there was also a tidy rosewood desk with only a white cloth on the surface that sat next to the door. I saw my reflection alongside Ras' in the full-length mirror which hung on the closet door by the desk. It smelled like cherry lip gloss in here, but I could find no reason or source for the scent.

"Please, sit here," Ras said. He stayed framed in the open doorway as he pointed to the straight-back wooden chair at the desk. It had a little seat-sized padding tied to the back slats of the chair but it looked completely uncomfortable. It made me wish for my Italian leather chair at my office, but I took the seat anyway.

He cast a glance at his uncle before turning back to

me and holding the box up near his stomach. "What I have here is something my family wishes my father had never found. But as he did, he is its caretaker. My uncle wishes for you to see it so that you understand that he cannot possibly bear the burden of becoming its caretaker. If my uncle is named as such in my father's will, you must make my father understand that the will needs to be changed. Someone else must be named."

So, it was about the contents of the will.

"Rasmus," I said, using his full name so that he wouldn't believe we were on terms close enough to be familiar with each other – he needed to know I was being professional, "I cannot disclose the contents of your father's will until he is deceased."

"We understand that, Ms. Hale," Ivar said from the other room.

"We know," Ras said, much softer. "But we think that seeing this will make you understand how grave of a matter this is."

He stretched forward making sure that one leg was always in view of the doorway as he set the metal box down on the white cloth. Then he straightened again.

When the box had been in his hands, I only had the view of it being metal. Now, I could see that it had originally been gunmetal grey and now was rusted in many places so that the metal was starting to flake in layers. There was a good chance that this box was older than the house.

I figured I was to open it, but I wasn't sure what would be inside. I had horror movie images of there being a trapped scorpion or a tarantula that would spring at me when I lifted the lid.

Ras had moved back to standing in the door and I wondered if he was trying to stay within his uncle's sight as if he couldn't "tamper with evidence."

"What's in here?" I asked, trying to keep my voice low and hopefully not echoing out into the empty living room. Had all the furniture intentionally been moved out so that sound was better heard rather than being easily trapped?

"Open the box," he said back. Surely his voice was loud enough for Uncle Ivar to hear.

I gripped the box and the lid, having to wiggle them back and forth in order to get the lid off. The contents slid back and forth and clicked against the sides. I was afraid of bending the aged metal until it crumbled in my fingers. The lid came off and I nearly dropped it in surprise.

Nothing jumped out at me but the box was full of pictures.

I set the lid down on the white cloth. My heart raced as I looked at Ras to make sure that he wanted me to look at the pictures. He nodded.

The pictures were old and most of them really small. Black, white, and in a few areas yellowing sepia. Corners were curled. I felt as if I should be wearing gloves to look at these.

"There's not enough light," I said. "I can barely see what these are. Can we please open the curtain?"

The stifling air of the house seemed to close in

around my throat. I needed to know the outside world still existed beyond this house. Seeing it through a window, it wouldn't be like being outdoors, but it might be close enough. And even though an orchard of fruit trees lay between this house and the road, maybe, just maybe, someone would see me and send help.

I had been in this house before. I could remember seeing the orchard out the window. There was a cherry and an apricot tree in the first rows of the orchard, and though they called it an orchard, they also grew vegetables between the trees. How did I know all this?

Ras looked towards his uncle before coming back with an answer. "Come over to the bed. The light will be a little better over there. If you need more, we can probably crack the curtain just a little."

I left the lid, but took the box with the pictures inside. I wanted to respect the secrets of the Kjelgaard family. I sat down on the dark blue quilted comforter covering the mattress, one knee bent so that my foot was beneath me and one leg extended out to keep my balance. I could now look through the door at Ivar. Ras had stepped carefully to the side of the door opposite the desk.

I went through the pictures without attachment. They were family photos and I had no relationship to any of the people in the images. They were all strangers. I didn't recognize many of the backgrounds. I didn't know what I was supposed to be looking for. Nothing I saw would change my stance of trying to convince Jens to change his will while he lay on his deathbed.

Perhaps Ras had brought me the wrong box?

"Look harder," Ras whispered and I realized that he was now standing with his back towards his uncle.

I knew I had to keep my head down so that Ivar couldn't see me speak. "I can't see these. I can't make out any faces. What am I looking for?"

I heard a door shut from beyond the bedroom and figured Mrs. Kjelgaard had returned from checking on her husband. "He is ready," she said to Ras. She glanced at me, sadness in her eyes, but a tender smile on her lips. "Has she seen it yet?"

"Not yet, Mother."

She patted his arm with her wrinkled hand. "I'm sure she will."

"Come away, Vera," Ivar's wife said. She reached out and guided Mrs. Kjelgaard out of the doorway.

"I don't understand what I'm supposed to be looking for," I said, feeling my frustration rise. "I don't know any of these people. What am I looking at?"

A door slammed and the house shuddered once more. I startled at the same time as I heard little feet pattering into the living room. "Beatrice must go back into solitary. She's been bad again," I heard Helga say. Then there was the familiar squeak of the cabinet door being opened, closed. "Are you done in my room yet?"

I realized I must be in Helga's room. The comforter on the bed did match the material of her dress.

"Not yet, my dear," Mrs. Kjelgaard said. "Stephanie hasn't seen it yet."

"Well, no wonder. You still have the light on. Can I show her?"

"If you think it would help."

Helga clomped her way into the bedroom, her bedroom. Her smile was big. "Rasmus has had a crush on you since high school. His name means *beloved*. Did you know that?"

"Shh, Helga," Ras said. But the blush on his cheeks let me know that everything Helga had said was true. He couldn't meet my gaze. I found his sudden shyness enthralling. Beloved.

Helga climbed up on the bed beside me. "Did they tell you that these pictures aren't of our family? Look at the dark hair. This is of the family who built the house. This is their box of pictures."

A load of questions entered my mind, some of them legal. Possession was nine-tenths of the law. Did the other family want this back? Was there a bargain made between Jens Kjelgaard and the family that had built this house that upon Jens' death, he'd return the pictures? Or maybe that the other family would claim the rights to the house back? There might be an old, lingering contract out there that the Kjelgaards now wanted me to fight.

"They hid the box," Helga said. "They wanted it to be a time capsule. Do you know what that is?"

I nodded. I remembered when they built a new school and they had all the students write a letter to future students and put it in a box which was placed into one of the walls. They'd called it a time capsule. As far as I knew, the time capsule hadn't been taken out of that wall and no one had yet to read her letter. I wondered if Ras had a letter in there too. What would his have said?

"They came around and told us they wanted the box back." Helga leaned forward and said this as a whisper as if she didn't want someone to hear. "We didn't let them have it."

A chill ran up my back at her tone. There was more to her words than saying that the Kjelgaards had turned the other family away.

"It's our house now and forever," Ivar said.

I looked up to see that Mrs. Kjelgaard and Ivar's wife had come into the room and stood beside Ras. Ivar stood in the doorway.

"This is our family home," Helga added.

"We'll do what it takes to protect it," Ivar's wife said.

I found myself returning to the pictures. There was something here in these images, I just knew it. Something I had to know. I continued flipping through them a little faster now.

The last one showed a man standing beside on of the cement stone pillars. It had to be Jens because the blond boy was in his teens and the photo in black and white. Stones lay around his feet. There was something inside the pillar.

I leaned over and with the tips of my fingers tugged on the edge of the heavy brocade drape to pull it open.

A sliver of sunlight came into the room and the image became clear.

There was a dark-haired man curled up inside the pillar. He might have been dead or unconscious. For every beat of my thundering heart, I hoped he was already dead before they sealed him into the pillar.

"Jens is dying and you will find that there is an addendum to his will," Ivar said from the doorway. "He has selected you to be the caretaker for the box and this house. You now belong here."

I felt panic rising and my pulse constricting in my throat. If they thought I was going to stay here, to be an accomplice after-the-fact to murder, they needed to think again.

And yet, this house… I knew of its haunts. Somehow, even if in a dream, I'd been here before. What other mysteries did this house hold?

"Jens is dying and we must keep the family intact," Mrs. Kjelgaard said.

"Always six of us," Helga said sweetly. "Like the pillars out front. It helps us remember."

Helga had been fathered to replace the son the Kjelgaards had lost, the one who would have been slightly older than Rasmus.

I suddenly got the feeling that they wanted me to join their family. Marry Ras and be happy. That's what they had said to me as a little girl clutching onto my father's hand as we came into the house. My beloved was all arranged. I belonged here.

I had slept in this room. The memory was coming

back to me slowly. Being roused in the middle of the night and leaving the house where I lived. I'd been in my pajamas. Mother needed to get to the hospital. Someone needed to watch me; I would sleep. Yes, put her down here. Dusty smelling blankets tucked in around me. The red digital numbers of a clock beside the bed. A hand brushing back hair from my forehead and kissing me goodnight, but it wasn't my mother.

I didn't remember what happened after that. I must have slept, but I couldn't say for sure. If I'd woken the next morning to the smell of breakfast cooking – something seemed right about that, but I couldn't say for certain – and clearly I'd made it back to my family. But a bargain had been made that night.

"Ras, she still hasn't seen it. Go turn out the light," Helga said, pointing with a wiggling finger at the light switch behind the door. Then she turned back to me. "It's hard to see, but once you do, you'll stay."

I think it was only a morbid curiosity which had made me stay this long. It had to be a desire to understand this creepy family. I'd never experienced anything like this with Jens Kjelgaard, and right now he seemed to be the only normal one in the family.

The light switched off, pitching the room into brown. There was so much light pressing against the thick curtains that even they couldn't hold all the sunlight back. Knowing there was sun beyond preserved my sanity. I would walk back out to my car, get into the collected warmth it had gathered from that sun while I'd been inside, and I'd drive away. I wasn't even sure if I'd go back to the office or home. Just away.

I could picture it in my mind; me driving in my car down the road, out across the desert, and into the hills that surrounded Little Grove. I'd keep going, and going. Then I was no longer in my car but flying over the hills and through the valleys, along the river, going… going…

"You're not looking at the pictures," Helga said.

"Leave her be, little Helga," said a man's voice from the doorway. "Her brilliant mind was travelling."

I would know that voice anywhere. I looked up and saw Jens Kjelgaard standing in the doorway. He wore dark luxury pajamas that might have been blue rather than black. In the dim light, it was hard to tell. Silver trimmed the hems and ran down the fabric covering the buttons. It looked so soft and I wanted to touch it. He certainly didn't look like a sickly man on his deathbed.

I stood, finding my relief at seeing him so great that I wanted to give him a hug. But I remembered that he was my client and I had to be professional. Or at least I should be. "Mr. Kjelgaard, so very nice to see you."

Then he was standing in front of me. I didn't know how he'd moved across the room so fast. His cool hands came to my face. "Continue traveling. Let that young, brilliant mind of yours soar."

"You need to look at the pictures," Helga insisted, and though she grabbed my hand, I couldn't look away from Mr. Kjelgaard. He had my full attention.

"Go on back to flying."

I felt a little woozy.

Ras was there to catch me. He lowered me back to the bed. His hands were strong but gentle as he guided me along. "You must have stood up too fast."

I nodded. I did feel light-headed. What would Mr. Kjelgaard think of me getting light-headed over just standing up? That certainly wasn't the actions of a brilliant mind. But when I looked up to see his reaction, Mr. Kjelgaard wasn't there.

"Your father?" I asked, glancing around.

"Yes," Helga says. "He really wants you to see. Look at the pictures."

The damn pictures. What was so important about those damn pictures? A man was dying – or was he, because he'd looked fine to me when I'd seen him just a moment ago – and no one seemed to care.

"I really need to get back to my office," I said, pushing away Helga's urging hands holding the box.

"Don't be bad," Helga said. "Beatrice doesn't like to be put into solitary. You wouldn't like it either."

The threat pushed me over the edge. I was going to get out of here now. If I'd really seen those images in the picture that I thought I had, then this family could be driven to murder. I'd call the sheriff. I'd show him the photos I the box. But if the family saw me trying to get help, they'd take my phone away. What would they do if they caught me trying to steal some of the pictures?

Help first. Once the sheriff arrived, the family

couldn't hide the box away. I needed to make the call and then stall for time.

"Restroom?" I asked. "Can I go to the bathroom? I really hadn't expected to be here for so long."

"Not. Until. You see it," Helga said with urgent annunciation.

"Okay, fine." I grabbed up the pictures in my trembling hands. I didn't know if I was more scared or angry. I had to do this carefully. This wasn't being careful. I started to flip through very fast. I'd fake seeing it. Yes. That's what I'd do. "Oh, there it is. I see it. Now, can I go to the bathroom?"

Helga hopped off the bed and put her hands on her hips as she stared at me. "You are being just as bad as Beatrice. It's time for you to go to solitary. Ras, put her in the corner."

I was a grown woman and it had been a long time since I'd been put in a time out. There was no way that Ras was going to go along with this. But he didn't laugh at his little sister. Instead, he reached for my arm.

I jerked away. "Ras?"

"She's right. You could have just looked at the pictures." His renewed grip tightened and he pulled me off the bed. "Instead, you had a temper tantrum about it. You need a moment by yourself."

I couldn't believe what he was saying.

"Ras, are you serious? I'm a grown woman." Stating it out loud made it feel like I was stating the obvious, but clearly these people thought everyone around them were like playthings who should behave as they wanted us to.

"Sorry, my dear, but yes, I am serious."

If he thought I was going to climb into one of the stone pillars willingly, he had another thing coming. He had to know this.

"Don't be frightened," he said as he ushered me around the bed. "I'll go with you."

He glanced back at his little sister, still standing angrily with her hands on her hips. "Helga, I think I better go with her. She might be afraid to be in solitary alone the first time. She needs to see that she'll be okay."

"Solitary." Helga stamped her foot. "That means she is supposed to be by herself."

"Stephanie isn't as brave as Beatrice."

I half expected to be led out of the room. I'd make a break for the front door if I had a chance. At this moment, I didn't care about calling the sheriff. I just wanted out. However that had to be accomplished, I'd do it.

But he didn't take me out of the room. Instead, we went back beside the desk and he opened the door with the full-length mirror attached to it. Behind it was a dark closet. It was large enough to walk into even though it wasn't a big area. Clothes hung off to the right and drawers and shelves were on the left. Coiled wire coat hooks were on the wall straight across. A couple of girl's jackets hung there.

"I'm not going in there," I said to Ras.

"See how scared she is," Ras said to Helga. "I better stay with her."

"I'm not going in."

Ras' warm arms wrapped around me and he urged me inside. "Stephanie, please?"

It was a whisper in my ear, soft, pressing, and urgent. He was part of this freaky family. But I hadn't seen him in years. Not around Little Grove. Maybe he knew that something was wrong in his family and had wanted away. What if he was trying to help me?

Did I trust him? No. Did I want to believe he would help me get out of here? Yes. Alive? Very much so.

I let Ras push me into the closet. I very much wanted to turn and fight. Or grab the doorframe and haul myself out of the small space. I didn't want to be in here. Not at all.

Ras closed the door behind us. "It doesn't lock."

I knew he wanted me to have the information, but it didn't make me feel secure. I spun around and found myself chest to chest with Ras. It was suddenly very much like the game where two people went into a closet for 10 minutes and during that time, anything went. Kissing, groping, more. I certainly hoped he wasn't in here just to feel me up. I tried to step back, but Ras must have thought I was falling over because he grabbed me.

"Steph."

I was not in here for a make-out session. I'd rather talk about getting out.

"We're going to have to whisper if we want to talk.

She's probably against the door listening," he said. "I heard something press against the door as if she were leaning against it."

It was completely dark and getting hot already. I felt the sleeves of the hanging clothes touch my shoulder. I wanted to use my phone as a light source, something so that I could see Ras' face and try to read what was going on with him, but I didn't want him to remember that I had a way to call for help just in case he was still siding with his family.

"All right. We're in here," I whispered. "Tell me what's going on? What am I supposed to see in those pictures?" Other than the fact that his father, my client, was at the very least an accessory to murder. Did he have a whole stash of bodies on his property or was it just in the pillars? Those pillars I drove by often. Did they wait until someone decayed to pull out the bones and whatever remained and then stick someone new in there? Did they want me to shove Jens' body into a pillar and seal it up? Was it a funeral ritual too? Oh, here in the dark, my mind was rampant with ideas.

"Do you remember the night you were brought here?" he asked.

Not until just a few minutes ago. "Yes."

"Your mother was very sick. She wasn't even going to make it to the hospital, and even if she had, they would have wanted to take her to a larger hospital in Reno. Your father had run into mine at the store where your father had gone to get some pain relievers for your mother before trying to take her to the hospital." His hands were on my upper arms and rubbed down them slowly, then back up. "He told my father what was going on and mentioned that you were already asleep and that he didn't know what to do with you. He really didn't want to wake you, but he also knew you'd be completely bored at the hospital while your mother went through tests. He didn't want to put you through that. My father offered to let you stay here."

Okay, I probably could have surmised that myself if I'd thought about it for one moment.

"But my father offered him something more," Ras continued. "He could heal your mother."

"How? He wasn't a doctor." As far as I knew, Mr. Kjelgaard earned his living off his investments and a couple farming technology patents. He'd always had an eye for the future. He'd once asked me about patent law, I think with an intention of moving his work to me, but I'd not gone into that sector of the law and had to turn him away. I'd wanted to live in Little Grove, be close to my parents, and there wasn't much need to patent law in Little Grove, or so I'd thought.

"He could heal her. He did heal her. Your father took the chance. She wasn't going to survive otherwise."

How was it that I didn't know or remember all of this? Had they done something to take it out of my memory? Or maybe I had just been too young to fully remember.

"Your father made a bargain with mine. You and I

were betrothed and a blood bond made between us. Let me ask: have you ever loved another?"

While in college, several men – boys, really – had tried to get close. I either couldn't open up to them or decided not to let myself get distracted. I was going to be a lawyer. Once I got there, then I could have a relationship and settle down into a family. But that was my own mind making that decision. Wasn't it?

There was a pause in the dark while he gave me a moment to answer. When I didn't, he continued, "But when you saw me, there was a pull. Was there not?"

Again, more dark silence before he went on. "You see, I had to be sent away. I too had to go get started on my life and figure out who I was. If I'd gone away to college with you or returned to Little Grove when you did, we would have been drawn to each other. The time was not yet right. I didn't want to wait. You've lived in my dreams. But I knew we were both caterpillars developing into butterflies. We had to be alone in our cocoons. Solitary. We were being created."

I scoffed. "And now we're alone in a closet together."

One of his hands left my shoulder and came to the side of my head. His lips brushed against my forehead. "Solitary in the closet together."

For a moment, I forgot how creepy this whole experience was. I felt his warm breathing, his chest rising against mine, his arms, his lips. Then we were kissing.

I let go of the darkness around us, of the thought

that whatever this blood bond was might be affecting me, of everything that didn't involve Rasmus with his arms around me. *Beloved.*

The light winked on above us and the door opened with such force that I felt air being sucked out of the closet. I winced in the bright light from overhead and turned, blinking, with Ras as we faced Uncle Ivar.

There was no mistaking his dower look for anything but unamused as he stood there like a disapproving chaperone. Thank goodness Ras' hands (or mine) hadn't been anywhere inappropriate.

"I think you should come on out now," Ivar said.

Ras stepped away from me and it became clear as I tried to follow that Ivar had only been speaking to Ras. Ivar held up a hand to stop me and hold me in the closet. Helga, stopping beside Ivar, held up a picture to him. Without looking, Ivar took the picture from her and held it out to me.

"I am told that you still haven't seen it. Take this." He flapped the photo in his fingers. "See if the dark helps you."

I looked at Ras, now standing behind Ivar at a profile and looking down as if he was studying something on Helga's desk. He was probably too ashamed to look at me. The thick photo paper flapped again. I took it from Ivar, half hoping that he'd allow me to step out of the closet now too. Instead, he shut the door and the light turned off with a heavy click of the push button switch.

I plunged into darkness once more. As much as I

wanted to scream and pound at the door, I fought the fear causing my heart to thunder and reached for my phone. Maybe they'd get curious about the silence and open the door. A normal person would try to get out and make noise. I waited to see if anything would happen. My fingers trembled as more seconds ticked by. I measured time by the throbbing pulse in my ears. While I knew that I hadn't even reached a minute yet, I felt as if I'd been in this closet for hours already.

The door didn't' open.

There would be a moment when they would open the door to let me out. Or, I assumed they would. This was a little girl's closet. She would need a change of clothes sometime. A dead body would certainly hamper that. Knowing that, I knew I didn't have long to call the sheriff. They would open the door.

In a larger town or even a city, I'm sure that I wouldn't have a cop's personal cell phone. Thank goodness Little Grove was small and everyone knew everyone. While there was bad about knowing everyone's business, there was also good, like having Sheriff Malloy's cell phone number stored in my contacts.

I tapped the screen and the phone lit, unlocking with facial recognition. As I turned the phone, tipping it slightly so I could for some reason also hold onto the picture, I saw something move across the photo. A reflection of the glow from my phone?

No, there it was again.

Photo in one hand, phone in the other, I used the light from the screen to look at the image.

There were orbs that came off the photo and seemed to float in the air as if I were looking at a three-dimensional poster.

"What is this?" I asked myself in a whisper.

The orbs would get to the edges of the photograph and would disappear. It seemed almost like they would come back into the image and start to inch their way through the captured background until they could burst forth again.

"What the…?" I started to lift the paper to look closer at it and all the orbs near the edges disappeared. The only ones that remained were those that were closer to the center. I tried to keep them from gliding off, something easier said than done, as I brought it up to eye-level The orbs were definitely floating off the paper. When I slid the photograph sideways, they all disappeared from the air.

"What is this?" I asked again in the empty closet as if I'd get an answer. This time, my voice was a little louder. But louder didn't mean that anyone heard the question or that I got a reply.

I looked back at the picture. Orbs were starting to squeeze out of the image once more.

People seeing orbs in photographs likened them to ghosts appearing. Who didn't want to think that their loved ones were around them? But I knew the amount of debris that regularly floated in the air and figured that orbs were nothing more than dust or skin cells reflecting just enough captured light to make it look like something mysterious. The words "clean air" was an oxymoron. Cameras could capture that truth better than our human eyes.

But this... I was watching these orbs come out of the photo. Even dust particles couldn't do that.

So what was this? Ghosts? Angels? Magic? I didn't believe in any of those, but here I was seeing the unbelievable. And they only had life – if that's what it could be called – when they were directly above the picture. The moment one drifted too far away, it disappeared out of existence. I couldn't even really be sure that they went back into the photo.

I raised a fist and pounded the side of it against the door. "Okay, I've seen it. What is this?"

There was no answer and the door didn't open. Maybe this was a test and I had to let myself out. I reached down for the doorknob, a cool rustic brass, and found it locked when I turned it. I jiggled it harder and tugged on it as if that would make it miraculously open.

"What is this?" I shouted again. I beat on the door some more. "Let me out."

Still, nothing.

All right, back to Plan A. Call the sheriff. Get me the hell away from this creepy family and I could forget it. It was probably some phosphor on the paper or something that would float in the air and glow in the dark.

Then disappear?

There had to be a logical explanation and the Kjelgaards were doing this somehow to make me feel like I was losing my mind. I would call the sheriff, he'd detain them, and we could search for answers. I would keep going until I had them and we had enough evidence to prosecute the family for any wrong-doings. Murder had no statute of limitations.

I opened up my contacts on my phone. Would they hear me through the door talking to the sheriff. Would they throw open the door and yank me out of the closet? Would I be dead before the sherif got here? These questions didn't stop my fingers from pressing his number to begin the call.

"The number you have dialed has been disconnected," a recorded female voice said back to me.

"Wait? What?" I said, responding half in shock. Why would that have happened? Why would the sheriff's phone be disconnected?

Fine. I could dial 9-1-1. It might be better for me anyway. If Ivar heard me calling for help and dragged me out of the closet, I'd toss my phone towards the hanging clothes, or even better up on one of the top shelves, and I'd fight him – the whole family if I had to – so that my call would stay connected and the dispatcher would know I was in trouble. Help would come roaring in.

"The number you have dialed has been disconnected."

9-1-1 does not get disconnected.

Fine. I'd call the office.

"The number you have dialed has been disconnected."

My parents?

"The number you have dialed –"

I dropped my arms to my sides and hung my head. The gentle, defeated swing of my arm tapped my phone against my leg. How could this be happening? What or who could do this?

I stumbled backwards against the floor and slumped to the floor. A shoe tucked uncomfortably beneath my thigh and I pulled it out. A little girl's shoe. The black polish shined in the luminescence from my phone. My phone which only connected to disconnected numbers even though I knew they were still in service. I was isolated.

Social media? Could I get a message out that way?

Every single page returned a 404 – Page Not Found message.

What would happen to me? How long would it take before someone noticed I was missing? How long had it taken for someone to realize the people sealed up in the pillars were gone?

Was Helga's mother in one of the pillars too? What had happened to her? What would happen to me if I couldn't escape? Would I end up in a pillar too? There were five of them around me in the darkened house.

Sweat came to my brow as the temperature in the room started to rise.

As quietly as I could, I changed the message on my voice mail. I didn't know if anyone else could reach me or if my phone number would somehow strangely be disconnected, but it was worth a try. If any caller got through, they'd hear that I was at Mr. Kjelgaard's house and that I needed help. Bring the police. It was the best I could do.

It was time to stand up, to start beating on the door, to do whatever I had to in order to get out of this closet. I would yell. I would scream. Until I became hoarse if I needed to. They couldn't keep me trapped here like this.

I rolled my hips as I started to get off of the floor and I caught sight of the picture. I'd forgotten about it and must have dropped it because it lay near my knee. The whole image glowed now and I knew it wasn't reflecting light from my phone which had gone dark once I quit using it. The light that I had in the closet was now all coming from the photo. It was bright enough and my eyes had adjusted so much that I could actually see the wood drawers and shadows cast by the handles. The upper shelves disappeared into darkness but even some of the lower hems of dresses and long sleeves were visible in the dim light.

I settled back against the wall and picked up the picture again. This was not the old photo I had originally seen but it had to be of Jens Kjelgaard standing beside the pillar. He looked thirty years younger than I knew him now. Behind him was a body inside the center of the pillar.

Little floating balls still came off the picture and they seemed to elongate as if stretching for me.

I pulled the picture a little closer. I needed to see it more clearly.

This wasn't a body inside the pillar, at least not a

dead one. No, this one had a woman. It was my mother. Her arms curled around her knees which were tucked in as closely as she could get them. She looked out. She was scared, yes, but she was alive and not fighting what was about to happen to her. Did she know her fate?

My mother was alive and fine.

But she had been sick. I'd been brought to stay the night with the Kjelgaards so that my father could take her for medical help.

I thought back on this time. I remembered my mother being sick. She was always so tired by evening. Medicines were always out on the counter within easy reach. She kept them close, taking more and more as night came.

I was taken out of my house in the middle of the night. The medicines were no longer helping.

Everything felt so foggy after that. I couldn't say I had any clear memories, but I'd been young. What I did recall was that the medicines started to disappear from the counter. Mom was no longer sick every evening. Something had definitely happened.

What?

Mr. Kjelgaard had offered to take care of my mother. Here she was inside one of the pillars.

Outside the closet, someone moved and the wood of the house creaked. I felt the vibration through the floorboard. Someone was walking down the hallway.

Whatever had happened that night when I was taken out of the house in my pajamas and left with near complete strangers, it had been a serious health predicament for my mother. My father had to be stretched to near breaking at the thought of losing her. He'd made a bargain with the Kjelgaards.

I saw my father in the photo now, his form emerging from the shadows of the image, but he'd been standing beside the pillar with his hand on it. I couldn't quite see his face yet I knew he had to be scared too.

"There it goes, your brilliant mind taking flight again and putting the pieces together," Jens Kjelgaard said to me.

The door hadn't opened, but there he was standing before me. His back was against the closet door and I had to put my head against the wall so that I could look up to see him. He was pale, nearly all white though I could still see the fancy black pajamas he wore.

"Are you a ghost?" I asked.

He smiled. "Nearly. I am passing over. What you see coming off the photo is bits of my soul."

I knew there were cultures out there that believed (and some even still did believe) that cameras sucked out a person's soul as captured the image. What if it were true?

"Don't come back now," he said. "Keep flying. Keep figuring this out."

"I don't understand though. I know these pictures mean something, but I don't know what."

He knelt and put his hand on my head. "You are beginning to see."

At his touch, I started to feel more than think. I remembered how quickly my mother had gotten sick and though I didn't have clear memories of it, I knew I'd been upset by it and I'd picked up on my father's worry. Mom was slipping away from us.

Then she wasn't.

Mr. Kjelgaard had helped. He'd done something. This picture showed what he'd done. Mom had gone inside the pillar and she'd come out healed. This photo captured the moment. Captured Mr. Kjelgaard's soul which now was leaving the picture.

What would happen when Mr. Kjelgaard died? He said he wasn't a ghost, but that his soul was leaving the photo.

"Will my mom get sick again when you die?" I asked.

"I'm not sure what will happen," he said. "Excuse an old man while I sit down on the floor with you."

Whatever this apparition of Mr. Kjelgaard was that I was seeing, he eased himself down onto the floor and as we sat cross-legged both of our knees touched. "A long time ago, I found a box of pictures. At first, I thought it was just photos of the previous family who had built this house, but then I realized it was something more. The front room which you think would make a lovely office – which it would, by the way – was once a meeting room for a secret society dealing with the occult. It was large enough for its members to have their ceremonies and the unorthodox practices. But Little Grove is a small town and word gets out."

I could agree with that. It's hard to have secrets

when everyone has known each other since kindergarten.

"The house must stay in our family. It can't go back to the original family who built it. Their way was chaos and the forces they were dealing with unnatural." Jens looked uncomfortable speaking it and though I had questions I knew I had no desire to answer them. I suspected Ivar would know and that a more comfortable time would come when I could ask my questions to Jens' brother. Now was not the time for that.

Now, I needed to understand the box, for that was why I had been called to the house.

"I have done many things I'm not proud of," Jens continued. "But I have tried to right my mistakes and to use what I've learned from the box for good. Your mother was one of them. I've done it for others, given people a chance at life. Every one of them feels fear. It's a terror to be sealed away, alone. What can one do when they are solitary and cannot reach out to another for help?"

I thought of my phone, useless in trying to reach out for help. Lines disconnected. Pages not found. I wanted to ask, but I knew from the orbs dimming as they came off the photo now that time was growing shorter.

"Someone must take control of the box. Someone needs to safeguard it and to become the next generation to help others. You have always wanted to help others and you are in a position to see the best and the worst of people. Your brilliant mind could use the box and better humanity, even by giving in to the true nature of the box."

He wasn't saying it, but I knew he was referring to the original purpose of the secret society he'd mentioned. So many questions I had. What were their unnatural and unorthodox practices? Jens didn't have time. I would have to, as he said, use my brilliant mind to find my own path with the box just as he had.

"If I don't accept, what will happen?" I asked. I had to know what I was going to be responsible for if I just walked away.

"As you have guessed, there's a good chance that all the people I helped will return to their previous states. Your mother might return to her deathbed. I am not sure which holds more power, the healing of the river rock pillars, or the photos taken as people are placed inside. I have never known which is the true activation, but I almost believe it is the photos. What I do know is that someone must sit inside the pillar and a photo must be taken. Beyond that, I am not quite sure how it works."

Jens closed his eyes for a moment, his head tilting slightly as a soft smile came to his lips. "My wife is here. It is almost time for me to go. It will be so hard to leave her love. Be patient with Helga too. She thinks she knows everything. She knows quite a bit, and someday she may take possession of the box if you see fit. For now, she is far too young and still has her life to explore as Ras did. I am sorry for the blood bond, but I wanted both you and Ras to be happy like my wife and

I are. Please forgive an old man for being a judge to ensure the future of his family."

Tears came to my eyes. I wasn't sure if I wanted any of this, and yet I was ready to come out of the solitary dark I'd been in for so long.

"There," he said, opening his eyes once more. "That is your mind wanting to fly. Let it."

I still wasn't sure. I felt a friction holding me back as if I knew that I'd become the scales of justice helping those in need and convicting those who were wrong. As an attorney, I saw so much of both sides. Who was I to decide?

"Do not fear," Jens said. "Trust yourself and who you are. You won't choose wrong."

He could feel it. He knew my thoughts. Somehow, he read my mind. Was it because he was near death and could feel a greater connection or was it because he'd faced his own fears when he'd discovered the box?

"Take the responsibility. It is all something we do in one fashion or another," Jens said and even though his voice was filled with conviction, I knew his words were true. In living, we are all responsible for our lives and every aspect of it.

He reached towards me and I lifted my hands to take his in mine. Here was my client teaching me more about life than I ever thought possible. It wasn't his hands that landed in mine. Instead, it was the jewelry sized, metal box.

And Jens Kjelgaard was gone.

A moment later, the door opened just an inch and I

blinked against the bright light and shielded my eyes with my arm.

I wasn't sure who had opened the door to release me. I waited for it to open further, but it didn't. After a moment, I got to my feet, picked up my phone and slid it beneath the box while I held the picture of Jens and my parents against the top of the box. Then I pushed the door open just a little wider.

No one was in the room. I took a couple steps away from the closet half expecting to be yelled at the whole time. I reached the door.

Sobs came from down the hall.

I stood in the dark living room listening to the grieving family and held the box just a little closer to me. If I wanted to run from the house, there was no one to stop me now.

The French glass doors creaked a little as if saying that they would open if I wanted to go. I turned to listen to the tears and muffled, but soothing words being spoken. As much as I knew that I wasn't family, not yet, I wanted to go to Ras and console him. There would be Helga and the widow too. A mourning brother and his wife.

The doors creaked again, a soft tap against the wood of the other. It had to be a breeze coming through the old house.

I glanced down at the metal box and the picture on top of Jens with my mother. Orbs no longer floated out of the pictures and I'm sure I would have seen them in the darkness created by the thick drapes covering the window. How many other people from Little Grove would I find in photos contained in this box? They were my responsibility too.

"It is time to call in the coroner," Ivar said to the people behind him as he came into the hallway. His gaze met mine but he didn't seem to be surprised to see me standing there. "I will make the call."

He took another door to his left and disappeared. Clearly, he no longer cared that I wasn't in the closet and he didn't seem worried that I'd leave.

Behind him, Ras came out from the far room at the end of the hallway. He'd been nodding and looking at the carpeted floor. When he looked up, he did seem surprised to see me. Surprised and delighted.

He wiped tears off his face as he hurried to join me in the living room. "My father just passed. We've got a lot of preparations to make now. But hopefully he's got all the legal items wrapped up."

"He does," I said. "Your father was well prepared."

Ras touched the box in my hands. "Does this mean…?"

"Yes." I took a steadying breath. "I'm responsible for it now."

The words terrified me. I didn't know what exactly that meant, but I knew they were true. But what made my heart really pound was knowing the next steps in front of me.

Both Ras and I had glanced away from each other, as if each giving the other a moment for the reality of the box to settle in. Now that the pause was over, we looked back. If I looked into his icy blue eyes for an eternity, would I ever really know him? Just as I had time to figure out my responsibilities with the box, I had a lifetime to learn all I could about Ras. In the back of my mind, I knew it was the blood bond that drew us to each other. Right now, I didn't really care. That blood bond had been the price to give me the precious years I'd had with my mother. Even back then, Jens had wanted me to be part of his family. A client has to trust their attorney to always do the best thing for them. Now, I had to trust my client. And in such an awkward, round-about way, I did.

It was time to throw open the curtains and come out of the dark.

As if he heard my thoughts, he stepped up close and took my hand. "Be my wife. I have always loved you and I promise to cherish you until the end of time."

The front room would make a lovely home office.

"It's time we move my car into the driveway, beloved," I said. "Wouldn't you agree?"

He took my hand, his fingers warm between mine. "I do."

A hiker finds a vacant cabin but her presence offends those who still decay there.

WWW.MORNINGSKYSTUDIOS.COM

Even ghosts
sometimes need help.

ALL SHE WANTED WAS TO ESCAPE HER LIFE.
WHAT SHE GOT WAS A HAUNTED HIGHWAY.

DAWN BLAIR
OXYGEN

SOME THINGS NEVER GO AS PLANNED AND SOMETIMES
WE ARE FOREVER CHANGED.

Half god - half human
Mysteries only she can solve.

WWW.MORNINGSKYSTUDIOS.COM

It takes a special breed to live
in Sun Falls.

Homeownership with a twist.

WWW.MORNINGSKYSTUDIOS.COM

Ready for Another Quest?

Sign up for Dawn Blair's newsletter to learn about new releases, hear about events, and more!

It's easy.

Go to **www.dawnblair.com/newsletter** to join the adventure.

Find Dawn on

PATREON

BOOKS AND ART

SUPPORT AND
GET REWARDS

www.patreon.com/dawnblair

Dawn Blair grew up on a ranch in a rural Nevada town. The old buildings provided inspiration for her imagination as she thrived on stories of unicorns, princesses, heroic knights, and hidden doors to other dimensions.

For as long as she can remember, Dawn has had a passion for storytelling. Though she started out writing, her creative life expanded into painting and illustration.

She loves creating worlds and spinning tales for people to enjoy. The best ones are the stories that surprise her as she's writing. She loves her characters doing the unexpected. She'll gladly tell you that the most exciting part about being a writer is being the first one on the journey.

Thank you for taking the time to join her on these adventures.

Find more about Dawn and her work at:
www.morningskystudios.com

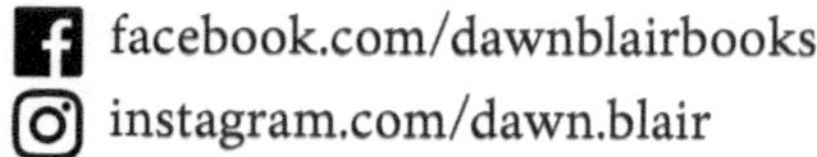
facebook.com/dawnblairbooks
instagram.com/dawn.blair